He swung his bat a couple of times as he watched the pitcher take his stance, and then he cocked the bat, ready. The pitcher hesitated, glanced back at the runner, and then glared at Kenny.

Kenny's heart was thundering. *Buh-BANG. Buh-BANG. Buh-BANG. Buh-BANG.*

"Make it be in there," Harlan was yelling.

"Don't whiff, whatever you do!" Bunson screamed.

But Kenny pushed all that out of his head. He watched the windup and waited for the ball. As the pitcher's long arm lashed forward, Kenny picked up that spot of white—small as an eyeball and coming hard. The first pitch was on its way.

Kenny swung with all his strength.

Look for these books about the
Angel Park All-Stars

MAKING THE TEAM

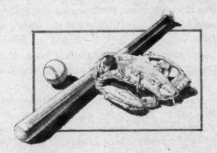

By Dean Hughes

Illustrated by Dennis Lyall

Bullseye Books · Alfred A. Knopf
New York

DR. M. JERRY WEISS, Distinguished Service Professor of Communications at Jersey City State College, is the educational consultant for Bullseye Books. A past chair of the International Reading Association President's Advisory Committee on Intellectual Freedom, he travels frequently to give workshops on the use of trade books in schools.

Library of Congress Cataloging-in-Publication Data
Hughes, Dean, 1943– Making the team / by Dean Hughes ; illustrated by Dennis Lyall. p. cm.—(Angel Park all-stars ; 1) Summary: Three third-grade rookies who make the Little League baseball team aren't immediately accepted by the older players. ISBN 0-679-80426-9 (pbk.) ISBN 0-679-90426-3 (lib. bdg.) [1. Baseball—Fiction.] I. Lyall, Dennis, ill. II. Title. III. Series: Hughes, Dean, 1943– Angel Park all-stars ; 1. PZ7.H87312Ma 1990 [Fic]— dc20 89-37926
RL: 4.3

First Bullseye Books edition: April 1990
Manufactured in the United States of America
1 2 3 4 5 6 7 8 9 10

for Kenny Hardy

★ 1 ★

Tryouts

Kenny hit the ball hard. When he heard that *crack*, he knew he had really tagged one. The center fielder ran fast, but he couldn't catch up with it.

Kenny tried not to smile. He didn't want the older kids to know how excited he was. This was his first time up to bat at Little League tryouts.

He signaled to Eddie Boschi, the batting-practice pitcher, to throw another one.

Crack. A solid line drive, right up the middle.

"Who *is* that kid?" Rodney Bunson said. Kenny didn't have to look around. He knew the voice. Bunson was a sixth-grader and the best player from last year's team.

"Are you sure he's only in the third grade?" Bunson asked.

Crack. This one was a monster hit. The outfielders didn't even move. They just watched the ball fly over their heads.

No one spoke as the ball rainbowed over the fence. Then Eddie Boschi, in a hushed voice, said, "I don't believe it."

Kenny could hardly believe it himself. This was a Little League park, but the fence was still a *long* shot.

He handed his helmet to the next batter. He tried to act as though he hit the ball that far all the time.

But inside he was going nuts. It was all he could do not to jump in the air and yell, "I'm going to make the team."

Billy Bacon, a stubbily-built fifth-grader, did the yelling. "No one can stop the Dodgers now! This kid hits like *King Kong!*"

The players standing nearby cheered. Kenny was embarrassed. He tried to get away but kids were crowding around him.

He heard one kid say, "He even *looks* like a ballplayer." Kenny acted like he didn't hear. But he knew he was big and strong for his age. He also had the steady, dark eyes of a guy who knew what he was doing.

Bunson pushed his way through. "What's your name?" he asked. But he wasn't cheering. He sounded angry.

"Kenny Sandoval."

Kenny was nearly as tall as Bunson, but Bunson had big shoulders and arms—almost like a man's. He looked mean, too, with floppy hair that hung in his eyes. He squinted so his eyes were just little slits.

"How'd you learn to hit like that?" Bunson asked.

"His dad was a major leaguer," Jacob Scott said. Jacob was Kenny's close friend.

"No way," Bunson said.

"Sort of," Kenny said. "He pitched in the majors part of one season. But then he hurt his arm."

"So you think you're a hotshot, don't you?" Bunson's face looked burning hot. Kenny had heard kids call him "Burner" Bunson. He was a pitcher.

"Lay off," Brian Waters said. Brian was little but he was also in sixth grade. "You're just afraid you won't be the star."

"Shut up, Waters," Bunson said, and he walked away.

Kenny tried to get away too. He wanted to take some infield practice. But Jacob grabbed his arm. "You're on the team for sure," he said. "Everyone says so."

Harlan Sloan, Kenny's other good friend, was right behind Jacob. "Henry White says you might even make the starting lineup," he said.

Jacob and Harlan were the same age as Kenny. The three had gotten to know each other over the winter, right after Kenny moved to town. But once spring came and they found out how much they all liked baseball, they were together all the time.

"I never hit a ball that far before," Kenny said. He smiled. "I hope they don't think I can do that all the time."

"Sandoval," a man yelled.

Kenny looked around. "Yes, sir."

Coach Wilkens was walking toward him. He was a tall, thin black man. He was smiling. "Is this your first year?"

Kenny nodded. "Yes."

"You're really only nine years old?"

"Yes."

The smile got bigger. "Glad to have you," he said. Then he told the boys to get back to their batting practice.

"Oh, man," Jacob said. "You're on for sure."

Kenny thought so too. But he told himself to calm down. "I still have to prove I can use this glove," he said.

He turned to go to infield practice and ran right into a big kid with red hair. BLUE SPRINGS GIANTS was printed across his shirt.

The teams from nearby towns usually practiced in Angel Park, where the league games were played. Angel Park was just a little California desert town, but the people loved their baseball. They had built a beautiful Little League park with four diamonds.

Another kid came over. Kenny thought he looked like a bag of potatoes. "We saw that hit," the kid grunted. "But you can't hit *this guy*." He pointed at the big kid with the red hair. "He's *'Heat'* Halliday—the best pitcher in the league."

"Heat" pointed a finger at Kenny. "No nine-year-old gets a hit off me. I'll stick my first pitch right between your ribs."

Potato Bag made a gurgling sound, like dirty water draining into a sewer. Kenny wondered if that was his idea of a laugh.

Kenny didn't need some guy throwing pitches at him. But he wasn't going to act scared. "Gee, I'm shaking all over," he said.

Potato Bag didn't like that. He made another grunting sound—like a caveman. Kenny walked away. Heat was saying, "You're mine, little kid. You're *mine*."

When tryouts were over, the coach sat down on a park bench and studied the notes on his clipboard. All the players waited.

Kenny and Jacob and Harlan sat in the shade of a eucalyptus tree. It was only early March, but the day was hot—like summer in most places. "I'm a nervous wreck," Jacob said.

Jacob was not very big, but he had a deep voice and a funny sort of face, with a gap between his front teeth and freckles so thick they bumped into each other. He could always make Kenny laugh.

"Do you think we'll make it?" Harlan asked.

"I'm sure we're the three best third-graders," Kenny said.

"I'm not talking about you. I'm talking about Jacob and me."

Harlan was big. He was fairly good at sports, but he crashed around like he was bouncing off walls. Even when he did things right, they looked wrong. He seemed to be made of elbows—and ears.

"We've just gotta make it," Jacob said.

"I know," Harlan said. "How are we going to make it to the real majors if we can't make it to the major league of Little League?" He flopped over on his back, crossed his fingers, and held them in the air. "I want to make the big leagues more than anything in the world."

"We all do," Kenny said.

Jacob put his hand up to his mouth as though he had a microphone. "Well, fans," he said in a deep, radio announcer's voice, "Kenny Sandoval will make his first start in the majors tonight. And his buddies—Scott and Sloan—will back him up."

Suddenly he changed his voice to sound like a slow-talking cowboy. "That's right, Frank. The young right-hander has a two-hundred-mile-an-hour fastball. But he *is* a little nervous."

Back to the first voice: "Why do you say that, Hank?"

"Well, Frank, I asked him how he was feeling and he puked on my shoes. I really wish he hadn't done that."

Jacob was always doing voices—anything to get a laugh. But Kenny was paying more attention to the coach, who had just stood up. Kids started to gather. Kenny and his friends headed over, too.

This was the moment of truth. Kenny was pretty sure he didn't have to worry, but he couldn't relax until he heard the coach call out his name.

He could see how nervous Jacob and Harlan were.

"All right," the coach said, "these are this year's Angel Park Dodgers. Remember, we only have one major-league team in town—and the league only allows twelve players on a team—but we have two minor-league teams. So everyone will get a chance to play. Next year, you can try out again for the Dodgers."

He looked at the little crowd of kids who had gathered around him. Then he read the names slowly. The first ones were older kids—most of them players who had been on the team the year before:

Rodney Bunson
Henry White
Billy Bacon
Brian Waters

Jennifer Roper
Eddie Boschi

The coach kept reading names. No third-graders. Kenny was nervous, but Jacob and Harlan had stopped breathing completely. And then the coach hesitated. Was that the end? How many names had he called?

"I always try to take at least a couple of nine-year-olds—so they can learn," he said.

A couple? Kenny saw the fear in his friends' eyes.

"But this year I took three. Congratulations to Kenny Sandoval, Jacob Scott, and Harlan Sloan."

"All *right*," Jacob shouted. He spun around and slammed Harlan and Kenny with high-fives.

Harlan was grinning, showing his huge front teeth. "We may be the rookies, but we'll show everybody what we can do," he said. He leaned back and laughed. "We're going to be *stars!*"

And then he dropped on the grass, flat on his back. "Bury me right here in the center of this park—close to the baseball diamonds," he said. "I've died and gone to heaven."

Kenny was feeling great, too. But he was

still a little worried. Brian Waters slapped him on the back and said, "Way to go, Kenny." But Bunson was staring at him with those squinty eyes. He looked mad.

★ 2 ★

First Game

Coach Wilkens had the players sit on the grass outside the third-base line. They were wearing their game uniforms for the first time—blue-and-white, like the big-league Dodgers. It was a pretty Saturday morning, warm and clear but not too hot.

Kenny had the new glove that his dad had bought for him, and he had gotten the uniform with the number he wanted: big number seven. He even had wristbands and a batting glove—the way most of the guys did. He felt like a real pro—except that he was *very* nervous.

The coach had put the team through some tough practices, but this was the real thing. Kenny was nervous, and he could tell that everyone else was too.

"All right, kids," the coach said, "I'm going to read the starting lineup. Listen for your place in the batting order and for the position you'll play."

Leading off:	Henry White, third base
Batting second:	Eddie Boschi, left field
Batting third:	Kenny Sandoval, shortstop

Kenny's breath caught. Jacob jabbed him with his elbow. "You're starting, man. I told you, you would."

Cleanup:	Rodney Bunson, pitcher
Batting fifth:	Jeff Reinhold, second base
Batting sixth:	Sterling Malone, center field
Batting seventh:	Jenny Roper, first base
Batting eighth:	Billy Bacon, catcher
Batting ninth:	Brian Waters, right field

Kenny couldn't believe it. He had wanted to play shortstop more than any position, but Danny Sandia wanted it too.

"I've tried to put a strong starting lineup together," the coach said, "but everyone plays at least two innings and bats once. That's the Little League rule. And I like to go a little further than that and give every player a fair share of the playing time. So don't worry—you'll all play."

Kenny heard Bunson mumble, "You gotta be kidding."

He saw Coach Wilkens' eyes dart in that direction. "You heard me, Rodney," he said. "*Everyone* is going to play—and not just the minimum two innings."

"I thought we were going after the championship this year," Bunson said.

"Believe me, we are," Coach Wilkens said. "We're also going to be a *team*. You older kids wanted to play when you started out. I let you have a chance and that's how you learned."

Bunson said, "Yeah, well, we weren't as bad as Sloan and Scott." Danny Sandia, as usual, was sitting next to Bunson. He laughed. Danny was a pretty good player, but he followed Bunson around like a stray dog trying to find a new owner. He even looked a little that way, with his shaggy hair.

The coach walked over and stood in front of Bunson. "You keep up that stuff and *you* won't play."

Bunson looked down at the grass. Kenny hoped that would be the end of all the trouble. Bunson had been teasing the rookies every day at practice.

"Okay, guys," Coach Wilkens said, "the Padres look pretty good. They're from Santa Rita, and they usually have a good team. Take nice, level swings—just like we've worked on in practice. We're batting first, so let's get some runs."

He stepped toward them and put his hand out. The players jumped up and huddled around him. The rookies got the idea and reached their hands into the circle. Once all their hands were touching, everyone yelled, "Gooooooooooo, *Dodgers!*"

"Let's get 'em!" Henry White yelled, and all the guys roared, *"YEAH!!!!"*

Kenny trotted over and found the bat he had been using in practice—wood, not aluminum. He liked the sound of wood on a baseball.

He was excited, but he was nervous, too. The butterflies in his stomach were starting to feel more like birds crashing around inside.

Jacob walked by. "Yes, fans," he said, "this is the day Kenny Sandoval leads his team to victory—and Jacob Scott leads his butt to the bench." Kenny laughed, but he didn't relax.

Most of the guys headed for the fenced area used for a dugout.

Billy Bacon, the barrel-shaped little catcher, said, "Hey, those Padres' uniforms are classy. They're the same color as something my dog did on the rug last night."

But Kenny thought the Padres looked good. The pitcher looked like he could throw hard.

Kenny also took a look at the crowd. The bleachers were almost full. People in Angel Park were used to great teams. The league was strong too. One year a team made up of the best players in the league had almost made it to the Little League World Series. Every year people said this might be the year they would go all the way.

Kenny saw his mom sitting behind the Dodgers' dugout. He wondered where his dad was. Then he saw him walking toward the fence. "Are you going to start?" his dad asked. He was grinning.

"Yeah. I'm batting third. And playing shortstop."

"Perfect." Mr. Sandoval was a big man, but he had a soft way of speaking. "Don't get uptight. It's just a game."

"Oh, yeah. Right."

"Well, it is." Dad gripped the chain-link fence with his fingers and leaned close. "Kenny, you're just learning. Don't put pressure on yourself. Just play—and have fun."

Kenny nodded, but he couldn't relax—especially when he saw Henry White walk up to the plate. Henry looked nervous. He took off his helmet and ran his hand over his hair. He wore his hair boxed on top in a "fade" like a lot of black guys.

Kenny sat down on the bench. Bunson leaned over and whispered, "Sandoval, because of you, Danny's not starting. He's mad, and I don't blame him."

Kenny slid away.

Bunson never seemed to let up. He and Danny had even given Kenny and his friends a hard time at school. Jacob and Harlan had messed up plenty, but a lot of it was because they were trying too hard to show Bunson they could play.

The umpire called the first pitch a strike. Sterling Malone jumped up and yelled that it was high. Bunson hadn't even seen it, but he yelled, "Come on, Ump. The ball was *way high!*"

Henry was ready for the next pitch. He took an easy swing and punched the ball over the second baseman's head.

He charged out of the batter's box and then slowed to stop at first. But then he saw the right fielder bobble the ball. Henry turned on his great speed, dashed for second, and slid in safe.

The guys on the bench went nuts. The season had started right.

Eddie Boschi—skinny but a good hitter—stepped up to bat. All the Dodgers were screaming. "This pitcher's got *nothing*," Bunson yelled. "Come on, Eddie, get hold of one."

But Eddie never swung the bat. The pitcher must have been nervous after Henry's hit. He walked Eddie on four pitches.

It was Kenny's turn to bat. He told himself he didn't have to drive the runs in. Someone else could do it.

But he wanted a hit, and the biggest reason was named *Bunson*. "Sandoval, don't blow it!" he heard Bunson bellowing from the on-deck circle.

Kenny's stomach was rolling and his heart was pounding in his ears. He took his stance

and breathed deeply. He pushed his batting helmet down tight, and then he watched
the pitcher and waited.

"Whatever you do, don't strike out!"
Bunson yelled.

Kenny threw his hand up and said, "Time
out." He stepped back. He took the biggest
breath of his life. He tried to forget all the
noise. Then he stepped back to the plate.

He swung his bat a couple of times as he
watched the pitcher take his stance, and then
he cocked the bat, ready. The pitcher hesitated, glanced back at the runner, and then
glared at Kenny.

Kenny's heart was thundering. *Buh-BANG.*
Buh-BANG. Buh-BANG. Buh-BANG.

"Make it be in there," Harlan was yelling.

"Don't whiff, whatever you do!" Bunson
screamed.

But Kenny pushed all that out of his head.
He watched the windup and waited for the
ball. As the pitcher's long arm lashed forward, Kenny picked up that spot of white—
small as an eyeball and coming hard. The
first pitch was on its way.

Kenny swung with all his strength.

★ 3 ★

A Big Hit

Pop!

The ball was in the catcher's mitt. Kenny had swung way late. This guy could throw hard.

The catcher snorted, then laughed.

Coach Wilkens clapped and yelled, "Come on, Kenny. Relax. Don't try to swing too hard."

Kenny knew that's what he had to do. But on the next pitch he swung at a ball that was up in his eyes.

"Sandoval, what are you doing?" Bunson yelled.

Kenny wondered. He didn't want to strike out.

The Padres' infield players were screaming to their pitcher, "One more, Izzy. Put it by him. He can't hit." And then they started chanting: "Hey, batta, batta, batta, batta . . . *swing.*"

Kenny let a high one go by. The next one was outside. Two and two. Kenny got ready. "Don't try to kill it," he whispered to himself.

High and outside. Maybe he could walk. Bunson couldn't say he messed up if he walked.

Kenny heard his mom yelling, "Make him throw a strike, Kenny."

Kenny waited. His insides were jumping and his hands were all sweaty. He wanted to walk. Next time he could . . .

And then the ball sailed right down the middle. It seemed to wait for him.

But Kenny never pulled the trigger.

"Steeeeee-rike three."

Kenny slammed his bat on the plate and then kicked up dust as he walked away. He couldn't believe he hadn't swung.

Bunson walked by him on his way to the plate. "I'll have to do it for you, hotshot," he said. He wasn't upset at all; he was happy that *he* could be the hero.

But Bunson didn't do so great either. He bounced a grounder to first. All the same, the runners moved up and then Jeff Reinhold, the second baseman, walked. The bases were loaded with two outs.

"Come on, Sterling, bring us home," Jeff yelled. Jeff was a round-faced kid with a broken front tooth who never stopped talking. He was best friends with Sterling Malone.

Sterling was strong and a really good hitter. He wore his hair like Henry White's— except that he had a part on one side. He clenched his fist and signaled to Jeff that he would do it. But it didn't happen. He hit the ball on the ground right at the second baseman.

That was that.

The Dodgers' big chance had come to nothing. Kenny felt rotten. But he had to forget it for now.

In the field, things went better. Bunson was firing. He struck out two batters and the third one popped up.

As Bunson walked off the mound, he yelled to the Padres' players, "You guys are getting *no* hits today."

"Oh, yeah. Just wait," the Padres' little shortstop yelled back, but Kenny didn't think he sounded very sure of himself.

When Kenny sat down on the bench, his friend Jacob came over and sat by him. "Don't worry about that strikeout," he said. "I do it all the time." He grinned.

Kenny tried to smile. He yelled, "Jenny, come on. Let's get it going." She forced the helmet over her ponytail and stepped up to the plate. She was a left-handed batter. Kenny could see in her face that she meant business.

And she *delivered.*

She hit the first pitch past the pitcher and into center field. The Dodgers started yelling, "This inning we do it."

But Billy Bacon hit a slow roller and Jenny was forced at second. When little Brian Waters hit a grounder, things looked bad—until the second baseman made a bad throw to the shortstop and the ball rolled into left field. Billy went all the way to third.

When Henry White walked, things were looking up again.

Jacob made his fist into a microphone. "Well, fans," he said, "bases loaded. One out. And *Eddie* is *READY.*"

"Yeah, ready to strike out," Bunson said.

"No way," Sterling said. "This pitcher couldn't get his finger in his *nose* without breaking it. We're all going to get hits."

But it was Eddie who looked like he would be lucky to do anything right. He was all legs and neck, like a crane, and he never looked like he was paying attention to what was going on.

Kenny was in the on-deck circle again. He was hoping for Eddie and telling himself what *he* had to do.

He heard the *ping* of an aluminum bat and looked up. But Eddie had popped up, straight in the air. The catcher staggered around a little, but he made the catch.

Two outs.

It was all up to Kenny now.

Kenny stepped up to the plate. He felt better this time. Some of the nervousness was gone. He shut out Bunson's barking and all the "batta, batta" noise. He just watched the ball.

The pitcher tried to sucker him with a high one, but Kenny wasn't going for it. And the next pitch made him jump back.

"Let him walk you," all the players were screaming.

But Kenny thought the pitcher would take something off his next pitch just to be sure he didn't throw another ball.

And Kenny was right.

The ball was down the middle and *fat*.

Kenny took a sweet stroke and lined the ball to right center. The center fielder ran hard, and for one terrible moment it seemed he would get there. And then the ball was past him, bouncing and rolling.

All the way to the fence!

The runners blasted around the bases. Kenny rounded second and spotted Coach Wilkens waving him on to third. He glided in for a stand-up triple. Three runs had scored.

The Dodgers were screaming and jumping around. Jacob and Harlan were going nuts. "You did it. You did it," Harlan yelled. "You're a hero."

Kenny glanced at his parents in the bleachers. They were standing up with all the other parents, clapping and shouting. His mom waved and yelled something Kenny couldn't hear. His dad just grinned. Kenny could see how proud he was.

Kenny tried to act calm, but he was shaking all over. Then suddenly he had to jump to get out of the way of a zinging ground ball that Bunson hit. The ball was down the line and into the corner. It went for a double.

Kenny scored and the Dodgers had a 4 to 0 lead.

Kenny yelled, "Way to go!" to Bunson, but Bunson stood on second. He didn't even look happy. His face was just as red as when he was mad.

Sterling almost kept the rally going. He hit a high fly that looked like it might be over the left fielder's head, but the guy got back and made a good catch.

Kenny grabbed Bunson's glove and ran it out to him. Bunson took the glove but said, "Don't start thinking you're the star. It was just one hit."

He walked to the mound. Then he yelled back, "Watch me strike out *all three* batters."

Kenny saw something that didn't look good. Bunson was trying to prove something. He was throwing way too hard.

His first pitch to the batter was high. Billy jumped for it, but it sailed all the way to the screen. His next three pitches were not much better.

When the batter walked, Coach Wilkens

yelled, "Come on, Rodney. Relax. Don't throw so hard."

But the Padres' players were getting on Bunson now, and Bunson couldn't calm down. He walked the next two batters. The bases were loaded just that fast, giving the Padres a good chance to get back into the game.

Coach Wilkens headed for the mound. The Dodger players were all sitting down. Jacob and Harlan pumped their fists to Kenny and yelled, "Let's get 'em!" but they didn't sound as confident as they had earlier.

Eddie Boschi was warming up on the sidelines. He had the idea that he could throw forkballs and sliders, as well as a couple of his own "secret" pitches, but they all seemed to float about the same. Kenny hated to see him take over for Bunson.

"Sandoval!"

Kenny's head popped around. He looked at the coach.

"Come over here. I want you to pitch."

Kenny's shoes seemed stuck to the ground. "Me?" he said.

"Yes. Come on."

Kenny got himself going. The butterflies-turned-birds were gone from his stomach now. They had been replaced by a flock of frantic bats—and it felt like they were banging against his ribs, trying to escape their cage.

★ 4 ★

Pressure

"Throw strikes," the coach said. He handed the ball to Kenny. "You've got the bottom of the batting order coming up. You can get 'em."

"Okay," Kenny said. He was trying to get enough spit in his mouth to swallow.

"And don't let Bunson bother you."

Bunson had just thrown his glove against the dugout fence and then kicked a bat out of his way.

Kenny couldn't worry about that. He had to think about the Padres. "Throw strikes," he told himself.

But his first pitch bounced in the dirt. Billy was lucky to block it. His next pitch took off like it had a mind of its own.

Kenny turned around and looked at the sky. He took a deep breath and tried to relax.

Henry ran over. "Kenny, throw strikes and we'll make the plays." He smiled. "Just forget anybody is on base."

Henry always treated Kenny like part of the team. And he was giving good advice now. Kenny told himself he had to do it.

But the Padres were all shouting at once. One big kid kept bellowing, "This little kid can't pitch."

Kenny stared at Billy's mitt. He thought of Henry's words. He aimed as he threw the ball, but the thing went wild again.

Kenny kicked at the mound, spraying dirt. Then he noticed his dad making an easy motion with his arm. Kenny knew what he meant. "Throw—don't aim," he always told Kenny. "Just act like you're playing catch."

Kenny took a breath. He didn't aim this time. He just snapped his wrist with a nice motion.

Strike!

The Padres' batter didn't move his bat. Kenny knew the kid was hoping for a walk. "Just play catch," Kenny told himself.

Pop.

Steee-rike!

The batter didn't move again. Kenny felt a lot better.

Pop.

Steeeeee-rike THREE.

The batter was the one kicking dirt now.

The next batter was a tall girl who looked more confident. But Kenny popped three strikes in a row. The batter ticked the last one, but Billy managed to hang on for the strikeout.

Kenny had to get one more.

The next kid timed the first pitch and pounded it straight at Kenny. Kenny gloved it and charged to the plate.

Force out.

The Dodgers were out of the inning.

"You did it again," Harlan yelled as Kenny trotted back to the dugout. "You're winning this game by yourself."

"Hey, don't say that," Kenny said. He could see Bunson sitting at the end of the bench with his eyes set straight ahead and squinted tight.

The coach was making substitutions now. Danny had gone in at shortstop. Kenny heard Coach Wilkens say, "Harlan, bat for Jenny and then play first base."

Harlan waited as both Reinhold and Malone grounded out. Kenny could see how scared he was.

Bunson said, loud enough for everyone to hear, "We won't keep the lead with that goof on first base."

But Jenny yelled to Harlan that he could do it.

Harlan tried. He swung hard at all three pitches, but he didn't come close to hitting one.

"That's okay," Kenny told Harlan as they trotted out to the field. "It's hard the first time. You'll relax next time."

Billy Bacon told him, "Hey, the first time I got up, the pitcher walked me, but I was so nervous I ran to third base."

Harlan laughed. "I almost hit that second one," he said.

"That's right," Kenny told him.

In the top of the third inning the coach put in Jacob for Brian Waters. Brian took off for the men's room, running as fast as he could.

"That's Running Waters," Billy said. "He always has to go."

Kenny came through again. He gave up a hit but no runs. And Harlan caught a throw from Danny for a putout.

Almost.

He dropped it, but he picked it up in time for the out. Kenny could see how happy— or at least relieved—he was. Harlan grinned as though he had made the play of the game.

That's how the game kept going. The Dodgers held the Padres to three runs—even though Boschi pitched the last two innings.

One of the runs was Jacob's fault. He let a ball get past him that he should have fielded. He also struck out twice.

Harlan also struck out twice.

But no disasters happened and the Dodgers won going away. In the sixth inning they scored three runs. Kenny got a big single with a guy on, which gave him four runs-batted-in for the day.

When the game was over all the players told Kenny what a good job he had done— all but Bunson and Danny Sandia.

Parents congratulated him, too. Mr. Scott, who looked like Jacob—small with lots of freckles—told Kenny, "You played fielder, pitcher, and batter, and did well at all of them."

Jacob whispered to Kenny, "He doesn't understand baseball."

The Padres' players were good sports. They slapped hands with the Dodgers and said, "Good game," even though they didn't look happy.

The following day, Thursday, the Dodgers practiced after school. Eddie Boschi threw some of his "secret" pitches. But most of the players had no trouble whacking them.

Then Harlan came up.

He told Kenny he knew what he was doing wrong now; he was sure he would start hitting better. But the best he could do was foul off a couple. He was so nervous he was shaking.

And it wasn't hard to see why.

Bunson was making fun of him the whole time. "Hey, Big Ears," he yelled, "if you want to help the team, bring a fan to the games and keep us cool. That's what you're good at—fanning."

Danny laughed, of course, but so did Eddie and Jeff and some of the other older guys.

The coach didn't.

He called everyone over. "You look good,"

he said. "You're the most talented kids I've coached. But you're not a team."

He stood and looked at them.

"I keep hearing you older kids giving the young ones a bad time." His steady eyes zeroed in on Bunson. "I'm warning you right now. I won't put up with any more of that stuff. We can be good this year, but only if we play together."

Kenny hoped that Bunson had heard the coach, but the next day at school Bunson stopped Kenny in the hallway.

"Hey, little boy, I want to talk to you," he said.

Danny was standing next to Bunson, frowning, looking mean.

"From now on, I don't want you pitching," Bunson said.

"Look, Bunson, the coach decides—"

"Tell him you don't want to pitch."

"Why? You can't pitch all the time. The rules say you can only pitch six innings a week."

"When I was nine, I wanted to pitch and the coach said no."

"I can't help that."

"Yes, you can. Tell the coach you don't want to pitch anymore."

"I'll do whatever the coach tells me to do."

Bunson stepped closer and took hold of Kenny's shirt. "If you stop pitching, I'll make everybody lay off you and your little buddies. But if you don't, we'll keep the heat on all year."

"I don't care. I can handle it."

"Maybe you can. But Sloan and Scott can't. I can have those guys going nuts."

"The coach said we won't be good if we don't play together."

Bunson pushed Kenny back a step—against the wall. Some kids had stopped to see what was going on.

"Well, then," Bunson said, "that's your fault. Because we're not laying off your friends until you stop pitching. Take your choice."

Bunson gave him one last shove and walked away. Danny gave him a push, too, and then he followed Bunson.

Kenny wasn't scared of either of them. But all day he wondered what he should do. Maybe he really could help the team by not pitching. At least he could help out his friends.

BOX SCORE, GAME 1

Angel Park Dodgers 7   Santa Rita Padres 3

	ab	r	h	rbi		ab	r	h	rbi
White 3b	3	2	3	0	Roberts 2b	3	1	0	0
Boschi lf	3	1	2	1	Jorgensen lf	3	1	0	0
Sandoval ss	4	1	2	4	Brenchley ss	4	0	1	0
Bunson p	2	0	1	1	Cegielski c	2	0	1	1
Reinhold 2b	3	0	0	0	Durkin 1b	1	0	0	0
Malone cf	4	0	2	1	Blough 3b	2	0	0	0
Roper 1b	1	0	1	0	Valenciano p	1	0	0	0
Bacon c	3	2	1	0	Brown rf	2	1	1	0
Waters rf	0	1	0	0	Shimer cf	1	0	1	0
Sandia ss	2	0	0	0	Nakatani lf	1	0	1	1
Sloan 1b	2	0	0	0	Orosco cf	1	0	1	0
Scott rf	2	0	0	0	Kim p	1	0	0	0
ttl	**29**	**7**	**12**	**7**		**22**	**3**	**6**	**2**

Dodgers	0 4 0	0 0 3	—7
Padres	0 0 0	1 2 0	—3

★ 5 ★

Turn Up the Heat

===

Friday after school Kenny and Jacob and Harlan held their own practice. Kenny pitched and the other boys took turns hitting. They also worked on their bunting.

They did pretty well, too. Kenny's dad had taught him a lot, and he tried to pass on everything he knew to his friends.

The afternoon was really hot. When the boys had had enough, they walked over to a fountain in the park to get a drink.

While Harlan was drinking, Jacob said, "Do you guys think baseball is as fun as you thought it was going to be?"

"Sure," Harlan said as he came up for air.

"Maybe we should've gone to the minor league," Jacob said. "We could have been the best players there."

"We'll learn a lot more this way," Kenny said.

"Right." Jacob nodded. "We'll learn to take garbage from Bunson. And I'll probably set a record for strikeouts."

"We're getting better," Harlan said. "I'm going to love it when Bunson has to admit we're good."

Harlan had a way of always forgetting the bad stuff—even all his swings and misses the day before.

Jacob shook his head. "Yeah, well, Bunson would never say anything like that."

"Maybe he won't say it, but we'll show him what we can do," Harlan said.

Kenny hadn't told them what Bunson had said to him. He was still wondering what he should do.

On the way home the boys walked through the little downtown area of Angel Park. When they passed the barbershop, Mr. Betz, the man who owned the drugstore, stepped out. "Hey, boys, how's the team this year?" he asked.

Harlan said, "Great. We won our first game."

"I guess you fellows are in the minor

league?" Mr. Betz knew all about Little League. He sponsored teams sometimes.

"No. We're on the Dodgers. In the majors," Harlan said.

"Hey, way to go. You must be awful good."

The boys smiled. "At least awful," Jacob muttered.

Kenny was still thinking. He didn't want Jacob to be miserable all season. The guy could play if Bunson would just give him a chance.

That night Kenny decided to ask his dad what he should do.

Dad was reading the paper in the living room. When Kenny told him what he was worried about, Mr. Sandoval put down his paper. "Do you want me to talk to the coach?" he asked.

"No. Please don't do that."

"But son, that's not what baseball is supposed to be about. Kids on a team should back each other up."

"I know. That's what the coach keeps saying."

"Well, if it keeps up, I'm going to say

something. For now, play where the coach tells you and help the team win. Maybe Bunson will start thinking about the team instead of just being the star."

Maybe, Kenny told himself.

"Dad, I can handle it, but Jacob and Harlan are letting Bunson get to them. If I could get Bunson to leave them alone, maybe it would be worth it. Pitching makes me nervous anyway."

"So are you telling me you're going to tell the coach you don't want to pitch?"

"I don't know."

"Son, I don't think you'd feel good about that decision. A team needs more than one good pitcher—and you're a good pitcher. But you're the one who has to decide."

Somehow Kenny knew that Dad was going to say that.

The next game was against the Giants. Everyone said they were one of the best teams. They had expensive new uniforms and they liked to act like big shots. They were mouthy, too.

The catcher—Potato Bag—never shut up.

While the Dodgers were taking infield practice, the guy yelled the whole time. "Hey, shortstop, you got no arm," he yelled at Kenny.

"Look at that guy," Jacob yelled to Kenny. "His uniform is already dirty and the game hasn't even started."

Billy Bacon yelled across the infield, "It's not dirt. It's all the sewer water that runs out of his mouth."

Potato Bag didn't like that.

Kenny had other things on his mind. He could see the redheaded kid—Heat Halliday—warming up. He remembered what Halliday had said about putting his first pitch between Kenny's ribs. One thing was true: the guy could really *smoke* the ball.

The Giants batted first and Bunson did a good job. He got the side out in order.

"Let's get it going," the coach yelled as Henry White came up to bat.

The Giants' pitcher took a slow windup and then *fired*. Kenny was nervous. "Heat" was the right name for this kid.

The next pitch was at the knees. Henry swung hard . . . and late.

The catcher gurgled out one of his laughs.

"Nice pitch, Heat," he yelled. "The batter didn't see it. He just heard it go by."

Henry gave the kid a dirty look, but he didn't say anything. And on the next pitch he swung and missed again.

Henry looked worried as he walked back to the dugout. "That catcher's a jerk," he said.

Billy Bacon said, "That's Herbie Crandall. I call him 'Cranny.' We went to the same Cub Scout camp last year. Sometimes I thought the wind was blowing in from the latrine, but I'd turn around and Cranny would be standing behind me."

The players laughed, but Kenny could tell they weren't feeling too sure of themselves. Malone had just taken a called strike that had popped in the catcher's mitt like a firecracker.

Kenny was on deck, taking practice swings. He heard Bunson say to Danny, "There's no way he'll get a hit off Halliday."

Bam. Firecracker number two. Malone stepped out of the batter's box and took off his helmet. He rubbed his hand over his flat-topped hair and then he stuck his helmet back on and stepped in. He looked determined.

"If he tries to pitch against these guys, they'll murder him." So they were talking about Kenny, not Sterling.

"He better not pitch, or *I'll* murder him."

Kenny acted like he wasn't listening.

Bam. Firecracker number three! And that was that.

Sterling was walking back to the dugout shaking his head.

"Good luck, little boy," Bunson said. Kenny walked quickly to the plate, trying to look confident. He didn't want Halliday to think he was afraid.

"Hey, Heat," Cranny yelled. "This is the kid. Remember what we promised him?"

Halliday nodded and smiled. He had big teeth, like a meat-eating animal's, and he was showing all of them now. He pointed with the ball—right at Kenny's ribs.

Kenny knew Halliday was bluffing. He got ready.

And then the ball was coming hard . . . *straight at him.*

Kenny spun away. He was on the ground before he realized the ball hadn't been that close. It was inside, but it wouldn't have hit him.

Cranny laughed. "Hey, whatsa matter?"

he said, as though he were talking to a baby. "Somethin' scare you?"

Kenny got up. He knew what was coming. The next pitch would be down the middle. Halliday thought he had Kenny scared and all he'd have to do is lay the ball in. But Kenny dug in.

The pitch wasn't quite as hard as usual and Kenny timed it perfectly. He slammed it right past Halliday's legs and into center field.

Kenny had the first hit of the game.

Heat stared over at Kenny at first base. "You won't get that lucky again," he said.

Kenny shrugged and smiled a little. He stood on the bag, like he was just happy to be there. But as soon as Halliday's pitch hit Cranny's mitt, Kenny took off. Cranny was taken by surprise. He hurried, but he made a bad throw to second base.

Kenny slid in safe. When he stood up, Halliday was glaring at him again. "You're gonna pay for that," he said.

Kenny shrugged again, smiled again. But he didn't say a word.

He looked up at the stands and saw his dad nod and smile. His mom was yelling,

"Way to go, Kenny." It was a nice Saturday morning, and Kenny felt great. He just hoped the coach wouldn't ask him to pitch. He still hadn't made up his mind what he would do.

★ 6 ★

Bunson Burns

Kenny clapped his hands and yelled to Bunson to get a hit. He could see that Bunson wanted to do something big. But Heat was coming with his best stuff now, and Bunson couldn't match him. Finally, on a mighty swing, he struck out.

Bunson got his glove and marched to the mound. Kenny knew he was going to try to show he could pitch as hard as Halliday.

But Bunson did okay. He walked the first batter, but he settled down and struck out the next one.

When Halliday came up, Bunson threw as hard as he could and was wild, but Halliday swung at a bad pitch and blooped a little fly right to Henry White at third base.

Cranny came up with two out. He tapped his shoes with the bat and spit on the ground—like a big shot—but he never swung the bat. He complained to the umpire about every pitch, and when he finally struck out on a called strike, he put up a big fuss.

"Listen, son," the umpire said. "I've put up with enough of your mouth already. I don't want to hear any more from you."

Cranny went to get his catcher's gear—with his mouth shut.

Kenny ran to the dugout. He was glad to be out of the inning. He hoped they could get something going now.

The Giants' fans were as loud as the players, and they kept the pressure on. One guy kept hollering, "Burn 'em up, Heat."

Henry came into the dugout clapping his hands. "Come on, let's get some runs. We can hit this guy. Kenny got a hit."

Kenny knew that Henry was trying to do what the coach had said—get the team to pull together.

But the Dodgers didn't score. Sterling and Jeff and Jennifer went out—one, two, three. Jeff at least hit the ball fairly hard, but the first baseman made a good play on it.

The Dodgers were back in the field before they knew it.

Third inning.

This time nothing went right. Bunson struck out the first batter, but the next one hit a fly that Malone misjudged. The ball fell in front of him and the batter turned it into a double.

"What are you doing out there, Malone?" Bunson yelled.

That was all the Giants needed. They got on Sterling, but they went to work on Bunson even harder.

"Hey, whatsa matter, Bunson? No burn in your pitches? Don't take it out on your fielders just because you can't pitch."

Bunson threw hard, and he did get two strikes on the next batter, but he ended up walking the guy.

And things got worse.

He walked the next batter on a pitch that he thought was a strike. The Giants poured it on. "Hey, Bunson, he can't *call* strikes if you can't *throw* strikes."

But Bunson threw one.

Piiiiiiinnnnnng.

The metal bat rang out as the batter connected.

The ball shot between Kenny and Henry before they could move, and it rolled all the way to the fence before Eddie could chase it down. It went for a double and three runs scored.

"Just settle down," Coach Wilkens yelled to Bunson. "Let's hold them right there."

But Bunson was mad. He threw the first pitch in the dirt. The runner took off for third and made it.

Bunson finally got a strike over on a three-and-no pitch, but then he walked the batter. And he walked the next one on four pitches. He had lost his cool completely.

Coach Wilkens headed for the mound. Kenny hoped he was going to talk to Bunson, try to quiet him down, or maybe bring in Eddie Boschi to pitch. But the coach waved for Kenny.

"Rodney," Coach Wilkens said, as Kenny walked up, "I think you've let yourself get a little rattled."

"I'm okay, Coach. I can get 'em," Bunson said.

"I'm going to keep you in the game."

Kenny was glad to hear that.

"But not at pitcher."

Kenny's breath caught again.

"I want you and Kenny to trade positions."

"Coach, I can—"

"Now listen to me, son. You've got to learn to do what's best for everybody. You worry too much about yourself."

"Why can't Boschi pitch? He's been working on his—"

"Because I just told Kenny to pitch, and *I* happen to be the coach. Remember, this is a *team.*"

Suddenly Kenny knew he had no choice. He was on the team, whether Bunson was or not.

Bunson kicked at the pitching rubber, and then he walked off the mound. Kenny started to warm up.

As soon as the coach walked away, Kenny heard Bunson say, "You just made a big mistake, Sandoval."

The Giants were yelling even louder. At least Kenny knew that a lot of the players in his own dugout were pulling for him.

Kenny knew he couldn't throw as fast as Halliday or Bunson, but he could throw strikes. And he could keep the ball down—

which usually forced players to hit ground balls.

The first batter was Halliday himself, and he could hardly wait to swing the bat. But he swung too hard at the first pitch and hit an accidental bunt. Kenny hopped on it and tossed home to Billy. The runner tried to score, but he was out by ten feet.

And then Cranny came up to bat.

He wasn't talking so much now, but he acted as cocky as ever. Kenny threw the first pitch right over the plate. Cranny watched it go by, and then thought of complaining, but the umpire gave him a hard look and he kept his mouth shut.

The next pitch was probably low, but Cranny hit down on it and bounced it weakly to second base. This time Jeff made a good play and flipped the ball to Jenny at first.

The Dodgers were out of the inning.

Kenny ran back to the dugout, happy he had held things where they were. He heard Jacob start into one of his radio broadcasts. "That's right, fans. The great Kenny Sandoval has stepped in and put out the fire."

And then in his cowboy voice, "Yes, that's

right. He just might be the greatest player for his age ever to—"

"Shut up, Scott," Bunson yelled. "Do you hear me? Shut your mouth. Those guys couldn't time Kenny because his pitches are so slow compared to mine. Next inning they'll be slugging the ball all over the place."

"All right, Bunson." The coach walked toward the dugout. "That's it. You're out of this game. When you make up your mind you want to play *for* this team, you let me know."

Bunson was on the edge again. Kenny knew he was about to tell the coach off. But instead he spun around and threw his glove at the bench and then kicked the fence.

"And stop your tantrums," the coach said. "Just sit down and be quiet."

That's what Bunson did. Except that Kenny saw him come close to opening his mouth again when the coach said, "Jacob, you go in and bat for Rodney."

"Me?" Jacob said.

"That's right. Bat for Rodney and play shortstop."

"But I—"

"You can do it."

Jacob nodded.

But Kenny didn't see a lot of confidence. He patted Jacob on the back and then whispered, "Don't worry. We'll do okay. This is our chance to show what we can do."

Jacob looked almost sick to his stomach, but he said, "Yeah. We'll show 'em."

★ 7 ★

Broadcast Time

Kenny didn't overpower anyone in the next inning, but he got three outs. A couple of balls got to the outfield—one right through Jacob's legs—but no one scored.

The Dodgers had to get something going. But Eddie swung three times and never touched the ball, and Kenny only managed to foul one off before he struck out. Halliday and Cranny loved it, and all the Giants really let Kenny have it this time.

What was worse, Jacob was coming up to bat.

When he stepped to the plate, the Giants' mouths started motoring. "Whose little brother are you?" they shouted. "Tell the coach you're sick, Number Six. Maybe you won't have to bat."

But then, just as everyone quieted for the pitch, Jacob began muttering to himself in that big, deep voice of his. "Well, fans, this may look like a bad situation, but it would appear that Halliday has begun to tire."

It was something Jacob did out of habit, especially now, when he was so nervous.

"What did he say?" Halliday yelled. He had been ready to pitch when he heard Jacob's voice.

"Nothing. Just pitch," Cranny yelled back.

Heat nodded and then stared in at the catcher's mitt again.

"Halliday has thrown a lot of pitches," Jacob announced, a little louder now. "He just doesn't have the sharp stuff he had at the beginning of the game."

Now Halliday could hear him. "Shut up," he said.

"Just pitch the ball," the umpire shouted to Halliday.

And pitch he did. He wound up and threw a pitch hard enough to knock down a fence. But it was four feet over Cranny's head.

The Giants' coach was yelling now. "Calm down, Halliday. This kid can't hit."

But Jacob was starting to enjoy this. He said in his cowboy voice, "I think you're right, Frank. He's losing his control. I doubt he'll be able to stay in the game much longer."

"Shut up, kid," Halliday yelled again.

Cranny turned around. "Come on, Ump. Make him shut up."

"You gotta be kidding," the umpire said. "You've been talking all day. There's no rule that says he can't talk too."

"Never mind," Halliday yelled, and he let fire.

The ball was maybe a little higher.

Halliday never got closer to the strike zone. On the fourth pitch he tried so hard not to throw high that he bounced the ball in front of the plate.

Jacob was on!

And now he was really having fun. He was flashing that gap-toothed grin of his. He went back to his broadcast. "Halliday has lost control of himself. He's so mad he can't think straight, and he's throwing the ball all over the place."

Twang.

Halliday had let fly with another ball that was over Cranny's head and into the screen.

After two more pitches to Malone, both balls, he turned and told Jacob he was going to beat him up right after the game. Then he threw a pitch so far outside that Jacob thought about trying for third instead of just trotting to second.

Two on, and things were looking up. All the Giants' fans—coaches and players and parents—were yelling to Halliday to calm down and not listen to Jacob. But Heat was only getting hotter.

The Giants' coach finally ran out and had a talk with Halliday. Heat did a lot of nodding. Kenny knew that he had promised to throw the ball easier and get it over.

Jeff saw it too, and he was ready. Halliday threw a soft pitch right down the middle and Jeff hammered it to right field.

Jacob took off with the crack of the bat, charged around third, and ran home. The right fielder tried to make the long throw to third and threw off-line. The ball got past the third baseman and Sterling came home to score too.

Three to two.

The Dodgers were back in the game.

Jeff had gone to second on the bad throw. Now Jenny had to bring him home.

Halliday was determined now. He made a good pitch. Jenny hit it and for a moment it seemed headed for left field, but the shortstop got to it and made the throw to first in time.

When the Dodgers ran back onto the field Harlan went in to play center. Danny Sandia went to second base for Jeff.

Kenny knew he had to do his best pitching. He moved the ball around and kept the Giants off balance. He got them out, even though the big first baseman hit a line drive that would have been for extra bases had it not been right at Eddie.

Things stayed the same into the sixth inning. The Dodgers had one last chance.

They still had to face "the Heat." He was pitching all six innings. The coach had kept him out of the game on Wednesday.

Eddie started out the inning. Halliday was back to his old self, throwing hard. But Eddie let a pitch go by and then took a nice stroke and just poked the ball into right field.

Kenny was coming up, and the pressure was on again.

But Halliday couldn't resist.

He threw the first pitch inside, trying to scare Kenny again. Kenny jumped back and the ball got past Cranny. Now the tying run was in scoring position.

Kenny dug in again.

Everyone was yelling—the people in the bleachers and all the kids in both dugouts. But Kenny kept his mind on his business. "Nice stroke," he told himself. "Just a nice stroke."

Heat blazed one in, and Kenny let it go by for a strike. He knew he had to get his bat around quickly against that kind of speed. But now he had the timing.

The next pitch was a hot one, but Kenny's bat was there to meet it. The ball jumped off the wooden bat with that sweet click he loved to hear. It shot down the line in right field.

Kenny thought he could go all the way to third, but as he rounded second he saw his coach standing near third with his hands in the air. Kenny braked and went back to second.

He had driven in the run. The score was tied.

Halliday was kicking dirt all over the place, and Cranny was yelling at him to settle down. No one in the park was sitting. Kenny spotted his mom waving and shouting.

Kenny knew Jacob was coming up, but he also knew that in Little League a starting player could go back into the game once the substitute had played two innings. The only thing was, the player had to bat in the same spot in the order.

Bunson was the only choice.

What would the coach do?

But Jacob was walking to the plate. The coach was sticking by his guns.

"Come on, Jacob," Kenny shouted. "Just like practice."

And Jacob tried. He took a nice swing and actually hit the ball—but on the ground and right at the second baseman. Jacob ran hard and made the play close, but he was out. All the same, Kenny had moved to third. Now the winning run was almost home.

And Harlan was coming up to bat.

Kenny glanced at Bunson, who was still sitting on the bench. Bunson shook his head, as if to say, "There go our chances."

The coach was also thinking. He was walking toward Harlan.

Jacob came running back from first. Suddenly he stopped. "Coach," he yelled, "before you do anything, let me talk to you."

★ 8 ★

Squeeze

Coach Wilkens called time-out. Kenny walked over to hear what Jacob was saying.

"Coach, let's try a squeeze play," Jacob said. "Harlan's been working on his bunting."

Harlan joined the huddle. Earlier, he had been red in the face from all the excitement. But now his face was white.

"I don't know, Jacob. A squeeze is tough in Little League. Kenny has to stay on the bag until the bunt goes down."

"But Kenny's really fast. If Harlan can push the bunt past the pitcher, the infield is playing back so far, I doubt they'll be able to get to the ball and make the throw home."

Coach Wilkens had his hands on his hips.

He was taking the idea seriously, but he was still thinking.

"You could have Harlan take a big swing on the first pitch," Jacob said, "and the Giants will move back even more. Then he could bunt when they aren't expecting it."

"Come on, Coach," the umpire shouted. "Let's get going."

The coach nodded a couple of times, still thinking, and then he said, "It's worth a try. Kenny, if Harlan doesn't get a good bunt down, don't take a chance. There's only one out. But watch the throw to first. If they mess that up, go home."

It was good strategy. Kenny went back to third. The coach talked for another few seconds to Harlan, and then Harlan walked toward the batter's box. He took a couple of hard swings and then he stepped to the plate.

Harlan looked awkward when he swung. The third baseman laughed. "This kid can't hit," he yelled to Halliday. "Just throw it by him."

"You wait and see," Kenny said to the third baseman. "He's going to hit the ball clear out of the park. He swings hard."

"Yeah, sure." But the kid backed up a step.

Halliday let fly with the first pitch and Harlan took a wild swing. He missed the ball a mile and almost fell down. All the Giants players started laughing. The third baseman yelled, "My grandma can swing better than that."

"Wait until he catches one," Kenny said.

"The only thing he'll catch is a *cold* from *Heat*." But the guy took another step back.

Halliday was smiling when he let fly with the pitch. It wasn't his best fastball. He wasn't worried about Harlan. But Harlan squared off and pushed a bunt down the third-base line.

It was perfect.

It rolled down the line, out of reach of the pitcher.

Kenny took off as hard as he could go. He knew the third baseman was charging.

He saw Cranny step up to block the plate. *"Hurry!"* Cranny screamed to his third baseman.

"Slide!" Coach Wilkens yelled.

Kenny dove headfirst and stretched his hand between Cranny's feet, reaching for the plate. Dust flew, and Kenny felt his shoulder crash against Cranny's shin guard. At about the same time he felt Cranny's mitt slap against his arm.

It was close but . . . "*OUT!!!!*"

"Oh, no," Kenny said to himself. "I should have . . ."

"Safe."

What? Kenny rolled over.

"The catcher dropped the ball," the ump shouted.

Kenny was about to jump up, but someone jumped on him, and then the pileup was on. All the players jumped in a heap on top of poor Kenny. But he didn't mind.

Everyone was laughing and yelling. "Way to go, Kenny," kids were saying. "Good slide."

It took at least a minute to get everyone unpiled. When Kenny finally stood up, he was grinning. Jenny was right in the middle of things, her uniform all dirty from rolling around in the dirt. She slapped Kenny on the shoulder.

Parents were coming fast now.

Kenny saw Harlan's dad, lanky like Harlan, hopping around like a bird doing a mating dance. He slapped hands with Harlan and said, "You did it, son. You did it. What a bunt!"

Lots of the players were slapping Harlan on the back, too. He looked as happy as Kenny had ever seen him.

Kenny spotted Jacob, and they gave each other high-fives. "Way to use your head," Kenny yelled in his ear.

Finally the Dodgers—with the help of Coach Wilkens—remembered to be good sports. They huddled around and gave the Giants a cheer, and then they walked by them single file and slapped hands with all the Giants players.

But Halliday wouldn't do it. He was standing by the dugout with his arms folded, looking mad enough to eat the chain-link fence. Cranny came through the line, but when he came to Kenny he said, "You got lucky today."

Jacob was right behind Kenny. He said, "Yeah, well, you told him he'd never get a hit off Halliday. What about that?"

Cranny mumbled that it wouldn't happen again.

Billy Bacon said, "I gotta go take a shower.

Cranny just touched me. I think the kid has fungus growing on him."

Kenny noticed that Bunson had stayed in the dugout. He hadn't celebrated with everyone else. Kenny thought it might be time to try to talk things out.

But just then he felt a tap on his shoulder and looked around. Heat Halliday was pointing a finger in his face. "Next time we *kill* you guys."

Kenny smiled. "Nice game. You're a good pitcher," he said.

Halliday hadn't the slightest idea what to say to that. He stared at Kenny for a few seconds, and then he walked away.

Kenny went over to his mom and dad. But the coach was calling the players together, and so he told them he would talk to them later.

When the coach got everyone together, he had them sit down on the grass. Bunson joined the group, but he still wasn't talking and he stayed far away from Kenny.

"Well, I'm glad we won," Coach Wilkens said. But he didn't look happy. "You played hard and you came through when you had to. I was proud of most of you."

The players got very quiet. They knew what the coach meant by "most of you."

"I just wish that I could get all of you to see what we're trying to do here. Baseball is a game. We play it for fun. But we also play it to learn. And what we're supposed to learn from it is good sportsmanship. Teamwork."

Kenny glanced over at Bunson, who was staring out across the field, not even looking at the coach.

"What makes this game fun is pulling for each other. That's what has to happen if we're going to have a good season."

Kenny agreed. That's what he wanted.

"So everyone show up to practice on Monday, and let's keep going strong. But let's all think about what it's going to take to be a real team."

He hesitated. "I'd like to ask the three new guys—Kenny and Jacob and Harlan—to stick around. And Rodney, too. The rest of you can go, and we'll see you at practice."

Team Members

Kenny and Jacob and Harlan sat on the grass and waited. Coach Wilkens had a long talk with Bunson. When it was over, Bunson walked over to them. The boys got up.

"You guys all played good," Bunson said. He sounded like a kid in a play—a kid who wasn't a very good actor.

"Thanks," they all said.

"I'm sorry I got so mad and said all that stuff."

Coach Wilkens was standing close by, watching. He picked up the equipment bag and turned to walk away.

Bunson whispered, "I hope you babies are satisfied. The coach said I had to say that or I couldn't play anymore."

Jacob shook his head and said, "Geez, Bunson, you—"

But Kenny jumped in. "Why don't we just lay off all that stuff?" he said. "You're one of the best players and—"

"No, Kenny," Bunson said. "I am *the* best player, and don't forget it. And don't think you guys are off the hook, either. You'll still hear from the rest of the team. I'll see to that."

Away he walked.

Harlan laughed. "It's been nice talking to you," he said.

"Can you believe that guy?" Kenny said.

"It's going to be like this all year," Jacob said. "It doesn't matter what we do."

Harlan shrugged. Even he couldn't see a bright side to this situation.

All the fun was over now, and Kenny could feel the mood change. The rookies would be the little kids on the team all year. Nothing was going to change that. Bunson would make sure of it.

"Yes, fans," Jacob said, "Kenny Sandoval was the star of the game, and Harlan Sloan came up with a game-winning squeeze bunt."

"That's true, Frank. But don't forget Bunson the Burner."

"I don't understand, Hank. He had a rather bad day."

"I wouldn't say that, Frank. He struck out three rookies without even throwing a pitch to them."

The boys didn't laugh.

They didn't even have much to say as they walked home. But as they approached Kenny's house, they saw something they hadn't expected. Most of the Dodgers were sitting on Kenny's front lawn. Kenny wondered what they were doing.

Billy Bacon stood up when he saw them. "Hey, do you want to go over to the school and take some extra practice?"

The rookies came to a stop. Kenny was about to answer when Jacob said, "Just Kenny, or all of us?"

"The whole team. You're on the team, aren't you?"

"Yeah. I just—"

"We all need to work on our hitting," Jenny said, "so we can do better against Heat next time we play him."

"You did great," Harlan said. "You got a big hit off him."

"Hey, you got the bunt down that won the game," Jenny said. "I need to work on my bunting."

"That bunt was Jacob's idea," Harlan said.

Billy looked at Jacob. "Is that what you told the coach? To have Harlan bunt?"

"Yeah."

"Great thinking."

"So what about it?" Jeff said. "Are we going to practice or not?"

"Sure," Kenny said.

"Hey, what's going on?"

Kenny knew the voice. He had heard it barking at him all day. He turned around and looked at Bunson—and Danny.

"We're going to take some extra batting practice," Billy said.

"Not until we get something straightened out, we're not," Bunson said.

"What're you talking about?"

"Sandoval isn't going to pitch anymore. If he does, I'm quitting."

"Why?" Eddie asked. "He's a good pitcher."

"It's not fair. A third-grader doesn't have any right to be a starter—and even get to pitch. The coach didn't let us do that in our first years."

"Kenny's better than we were," Jenny said.

"He's better than *you* were, but not better than me."

"Look, Bunson, what difference does it make?" Billy said. "He saved us today after *you* got in trouble."

"Shut up, Bacon. If he pitches, I'm gone. And you guys will be *nothing* without me."

No one said anything for several seconds. Kenny could see that they were thinking. They were all used to Bunson telling them how things would be.

But then Brian Waters spoke up. "That's okay. Quit. We'll have a better season without you—even if we lose some games."

"That's right," Jenny said. "Go ahead and quit."

"Yeah," Eddie said.

"Quit if you want," Henry said. "We don't care."

"You guys just don't think I'll really do it," Bunson said. His face was red—burning hot.

"We don't *care* if you do," Billy said. "You ruin all the fun anyway."

"You're a bunch of jerks," Bunson said. "I wouldn't play with you for anything." He stood for a moment and looked at everyone, as though he thought they would change their minds—but then he walked away.

"I'm quitting too," Danny said, and he followed Bunson.

No one said a word until the two of them had walked past the next house, and then Billy said, "Bunson won't quit. The only thing he cares about is baseball."

"That's not true. He also likes bossing people around," Eddie said.

"Yeah. But he won't quit. Let's go do some batting. Kenny, you can pitch."

Everyone laughed.

"You guys go ahead," Kenny said. "Jacob and Harlan and I will be over in a few minutes. We have to do something for just a sec."

And so the other kids left. Kenny said, "Come here," to his friends. He walked around to the backyard, with Jacob and Harlan following. They looked curious when Kenny turned around.

He tried to look as serious as he could. "Well, guys, I don't know if you realized it," he said, and he tried to sound like he had bad news, "but we just *MADE THE TEAM!*"

He grinned and held his hand out.

Jacob held out his hand, too, and so did Harlan, and then they all leaped as high as they could—for a big, *TRIPLE* high-five.

When they landed they looked at each other and laughed.

"Well, Frank," Jacob announced, "these kids are headed for the big time."

"I gotta agree with you, Hank. There's no stopping them now. But they better get their fannies over to practice instead of just standing around talking about how good they are."

And the other rookies agreed. But Kenny held out his hand again, and they all jumped up for one more flying high-five—just for the plain old joy of it.

BOX SCORE, GAME 2

Blue Springs Giants 3   Angel Park Dodgers 4

	ab	r	h	rbi		ab	r	h	rbi
Weight 3b	3	1	2	0	White 3b	3	0	0	0
Nugent lf	3	1	0	0	Boschi lf	3	1	1	0
Sanchez ss	2	0	1	3	Sandoval ss	4	1	2	1
Glenn 1b	1	0	0	0	Bunson p	1	0	0	0
Cooper 2b	1	0	0	0	Malone cf	1	1	0	0
Halliday p	3	0	1	0	Reinhold 2b	2	0	1	1
Crandall c	3	0	0	0	Roper 1b	2	0	0	0
Zonn rf	1	0	0	0	Bacon c	2	0	0	0
Dodero cf	1	1	1	0	Waters rf	2	0	0	0
Hausberg p	1	0	0	0	Sandia ss	1	0	0	0
Villareal 2b	2	0	0	0	Sloan 1b	1	0	1	1
Spinner cf	1	0	0	0	Scott ss	1	1	0	0
ttl	**22**	**3**	**5**	**3**		**23**	**4**	**5**	**3**

Giants   0 0 3   0 0 0—3
Dodgers   0 0 0   2 0 2—4

League standings after two games:

Dodgers   2–0
Reds   2–0
Padres   1–1
Giants   1–1
Mariners   0–2
A's   0–2

First-game scores:

Dodgers	7	Padres	3
Giants	13	Mariners	2
Reds	9	A's	1

Second-game scores:

Dodgers	4	Giants	3
Reds	16	Mariners	2
Padres	10	A's	6

ANGEL PARK ALL-STARS #2

Big Base Hit
by Dean Hughes
Harlan really needs one—or he may be off the team!

His buddies Kenny and Jacob, the other third graders on the team, have already gotten their hits. Harlan knows he won't really feel like an Angel Park Dodger until he gets his. But no dice—the harder he tries, the worse it gets. Soon everyone's starting to worry, especially Harlan. What if he never gets a hit? What if he doesn't belong on the team after all?

FIRST TIME IN PRINT!

For more fun-filled sports action, read the up-coming adventures of the Angel Park All-Stars™:

BULLSEYE BOOKS PUBLISHED BY ALFRED A KNOPF

ENTER THE ANGEL PARK ALL-STARS SWEEPSTAKES!

- The Grand Prize: a trip for four to the 1991 All-Star Game in Toronto
- 25 First Prizes: Louisville Slugger Little League bat personalized with the winner's name and the Angel Park All-Stars logo

See official entry rules below.

OFFICIAL RULES—NO PURCHASE NECESSARY

1. On an official entry form print your name, address, zip code, age, and the answer to the following question: What are the names of the three main characters in the Angel Park All-Stars books? The information needed to answer this question can be found in any of the Angel Park All-Stars books, or you may obtain an entry form, a set of rules, and the answer to the question by writing to: Angel Park Request, P.O. Box 3352, Syosset, NY 11775-3352. Each request must be mailed separately and must be received by November 1, 1990.

2. Enter as often as you wish, but each entry must be mailed separately to: ANGEL PARK ALL-STARS SWEEPSTAKES, P.O. Box 3335, Syosset, NY 11775-3335. No mechanically reproduced entries will be accepted. All entries must be received by December 1, 1990.

3. **Winners will be selected, from among correct entries received, in a random drawing conducted by National Judging Institute, Inc., an independent judging organization whose decisions are final on all matters relating to this sweepstakes. All prizes will be awarded and winners notified by mail. Prizes are nontransferable, and no substitutions or cash equivalents are allowed. Taxes, if any, are the responsibility of the individual winners. Winners may be asked to verify address or execute an affidavit of eligibility and release. No responsibility is assumed for lost, misdirected, or late entries or mail. Grand Prize consists of a three-day/two-night trip for a family of four to the 1991 All-Star Game in Toronto, Canada, including round-trip air transportation, hotel accommodations, game tickets, hotel-to-airport and hotel-to-game transfers, and breakfasts and dinners. In the event the trip is won by a minor, it will be awarded in the name of a parent or legal guardian. Trip must be taken on date specified or the prize will be forfeited and an alternate winner selected. RANDOM HOUSE, INC., and its affiliates reserve the right to use the prize winners' names and likenesses in any promotional activities relating to this sweepstakes without further compensation to the winners.**

4. Sweepstakes open to residents of the U.S. and Canada, except for the Province of Quebec. Employees and their families of RANDOM HOUSE, INC., and its affiliates, subsidiaries, advertising agencies, and retailers, and Don Jagoda Associates, Inc., may not enter. This offer is void wherever prohibited, and subject to all federal, state, and local laws.

5. For a list of winners, send a stamped, self-addressed envelope to: ANGEL PARK WINNERS, P.O. Box 3347, Syosset, NY 11775-3347.

··

Angel Park All-Stars Sweepstakes Official Entry Form

Name:_____ Age: _____
(Please Print)

Address_____

City/State/Zip:_____

What are the names of the three main characters in the Angel Park All-Stars books?

_____